# A Note from the Author

Fred and his merry band flew through me and onto these pages like my hair was on fire...

I realized – and quite quickly – that I over-parented my children. I talked way too much and listened far too little. I made the answer more important than the questions, when in fact, I see it clearly now: the answers are far less important.

These books are about encouraging children and their parents to be willing to ask questions...then to listen and know that the answers themselves aren't so important. Each of us has our own answers as life moves forward – like ourselves – our answers are subject to change.

My intent is not to go into my own versions of situational modeling; it is to inspire children to do that for themselves. It is for children and their parents to have original thoughts unique to themselves, related to their lives, to use their imaginations, to ask questions...

...and to have fun in the process.

Enjoy,
Kay E. Oswalt

To Lorne "Smokie"

You inspired me to find what it is I love, what it is I'm passionate about and then to do it like no matter what, I'd still do it...for free.

To Tegan, Dalton, & Skylar
For helping me to believe in endless possibilities.

To Dad, just cause...

# Fred Threads™

## book one: "the Interview"

book two: "The Boss?"

book three: "Big Trouble?"

Go to www.fredthreads.com for more info on the release dates of future "Fred Threads."™

Edited by: Christine Larsen

ISBN: 978-1-4624-0070-6 (hbk)
Library of Congress Control Number: 2012932468

Inspiring Voices books may be ordered through booksellers or by contacting:

Inspiring Voices
1663 Liberty Drive
Bloomington, IN 47403
www.inspiringvoices.com
1-(866) 697-5313

Printed in the United States of America by BookMasters, Inc
Ashland OH
May 2012
M9543

Inspiring Voices rev. date: 4/12/2012

"Fred Threads is an innovative piece of children's literature. Its beautiful presentation of the lessons it teaches, is worthy of every parent and teachers attention."

Wm. W. Oswalt, Ed D.

"He likes his mom."

Mikayla (age 2)

"THREADS offers a way to explore the many facets of love, caring and understanding the many complex relationships children encounter. What fun Fred's readers will have!"

Alma Schlenker, Ed D.

"The vibrant colors and rich textures in Fred Threads illustrate the author's simple confirmation of the bonds in parenting. Its captivating design is sure to pique your interest and the content will continue to surprise you."

Donna P. Nagle, M.A. Art Ed.

"Fred Threads is a delightful story whose beautiful illustrations depict its message about the importance of dialoguing with our children to encourage them to think critically and discover their strengths."

-Maria Palombo Murphy, PsyD

1

Mom~~

I have to interview someone
for Language class.

Can I interview you?

Sure, Fred, that would be fun!

Great! Mom, what do you
do for a living?

I'm an artist. I paint, I draw, I sculpt and I make jewelry.

4

Where do you work?

I work from home.

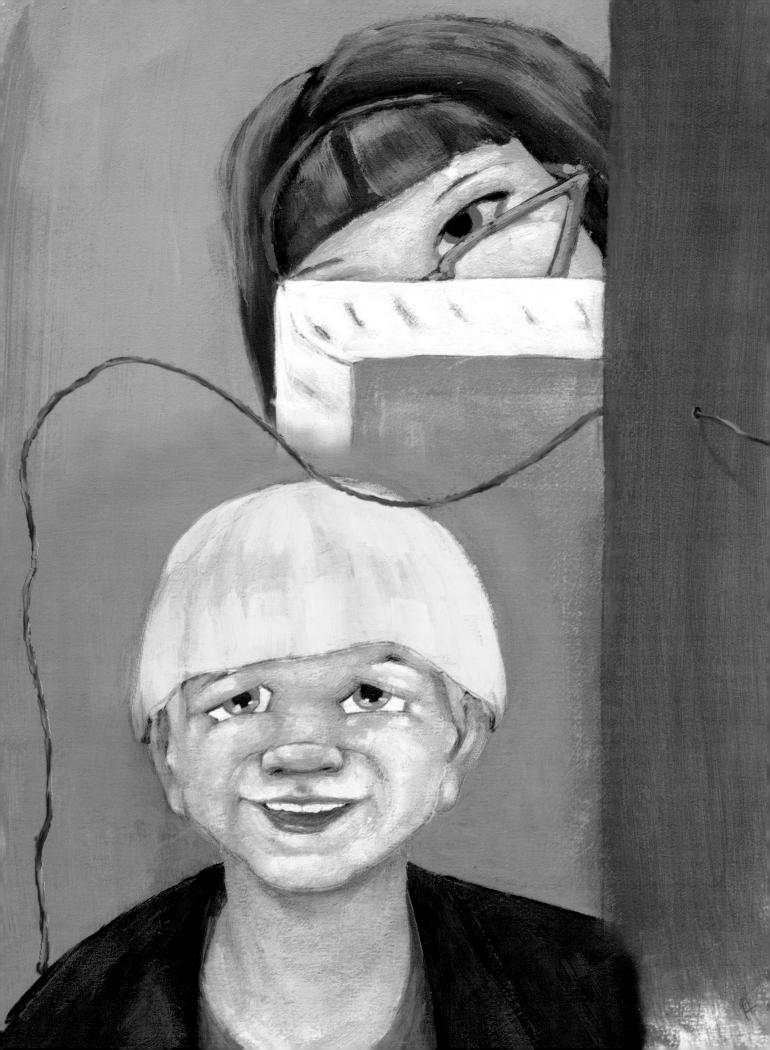

Do you like what you do?

I love it, Fred!

Do people buy what you make?

Yes, I sell what I make to people, here from home and at Jane's Gallery in town.

Mom~~~

Did you always want to be an artist?

At one time Fred, I wanted to be a doctor.

Why did you choose to be an artist then?

Well, Fred, because I was just plain better
at being an artist than a doctor.

14

Oh...so-o-o-
painting was a
bigger and better
choice for you?

15

Yes, Fred, it definitely was.

16

Hm~m~m~m...So, Mom, were you following one of your own rules?

I guess you could say that, Fred.

Can you tell me the rule, Mom?

To do what makes me happy, Fred. And, that meant to do something I was good at.

So, Mom, do you always know the right things to do and the right things to say?

Oh no, Fred, I don't.

You seem to, Mom.

Fred, I listen and I ask questions ~ just like you are doing right now.

So, Mom, asking questions is important?
I believe so, yes, Fred.

Why, Mom?

The questions, Fred, help me gather information when I want to know something.

So you can make bigger and better choices Mom!?

Yes, Fred exactly!

www.fredthreads.com

Mom~~

I'm really glad you chose
to marry Dad!

You ar-r-r-e-e??

Yeah~h~h~h! Because then you had me!

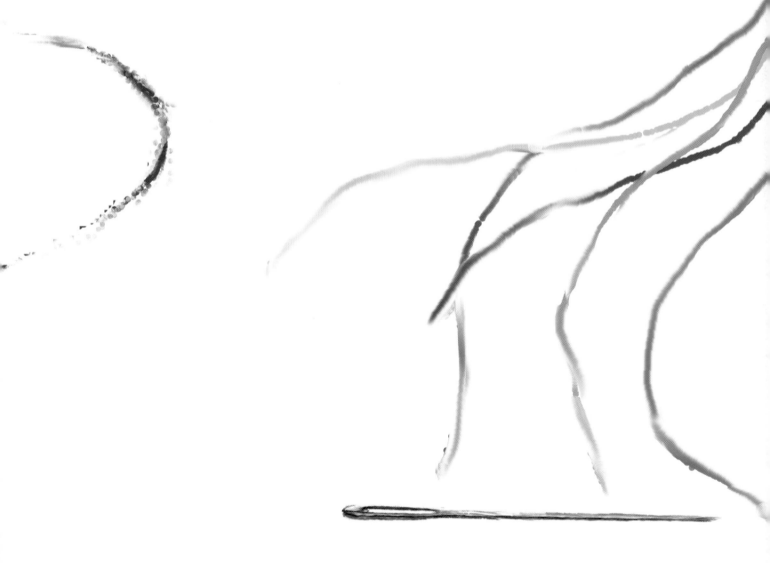

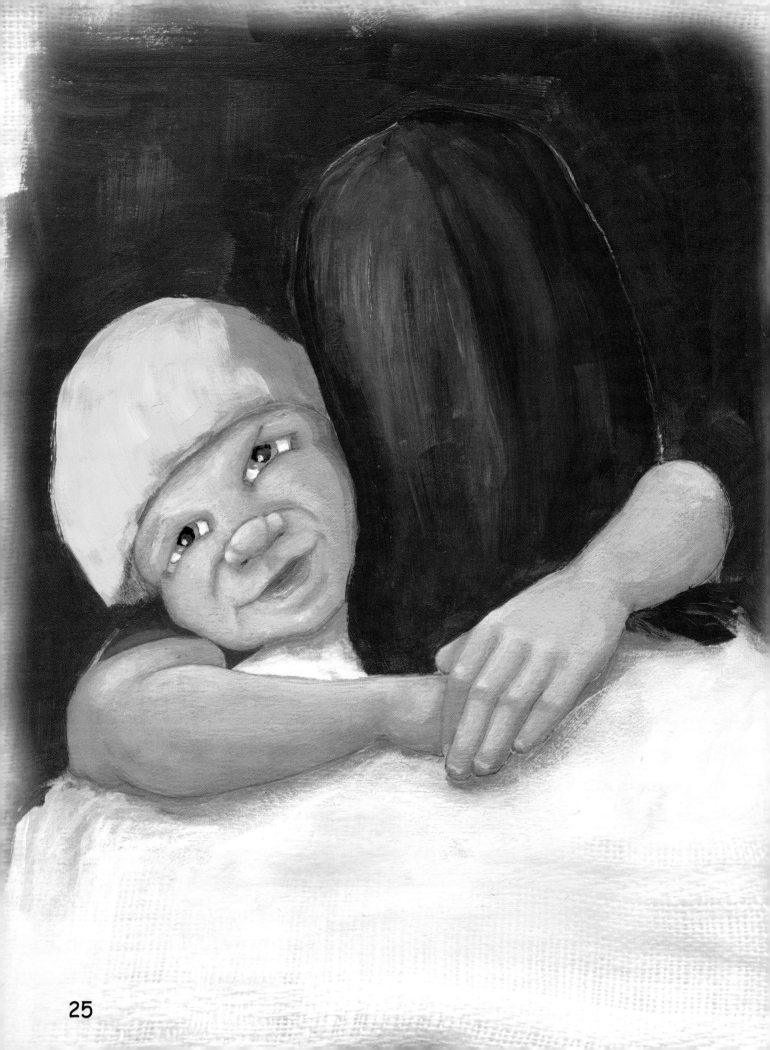

THAT was a great choice, Fred!

Yes, it was, Mom!

Mom~~
I love you.

Oh, Fred, I love you too.

It has been said

Our children hold our hands

For such a short time.

So we nurture, we cherish

We kiss those bruised knees.

And, we know there is truth in:

Mom~~~

You're not the boss of me!

Kay E. Oswalt

# Discussion Points:

1. What does this story make you think of?

2. What choice did you make today?
...and, how did you come to that choice?

3. Who would you like to interview?  Why?

"Questioning and critical thinking are essential skills that help all of us gather information and construct meaning. "Fred Threads" leads children on a meaningful journey, stitch together ideas, ask questions and make connections to their world in order to make informed choices."

Carol J. Allen, M Ed.
"Reading Specialist"

## Illustrator's Notes:

Illustrating Fred is a wonderful experience. It is my hope the images illuminate our gentle rituals of childhood and parenting.

Paul Nagle

for Donna, Milo, and Thea, my threads through life.

VII